An Unwelcome Visitor!

The great white shark swims slowly toward you, moving side-to-side so that each eye can size you up and each nostril can smell you. Your eyes widen when you see its full length of about thirty feet.

The shark swims around in a circle. Now it seems to smell something appetizing. Blood. It comes back for a second look, this time with its jaws wide open.

For a split second dozens of gleaming white teeth flash in the sunlight. Each one is two or three inches long. And that's the last thing you see as the shark swallows you whole!

EXPLORER™

Adventure on the Frontiers of Science.

#3

IN SEARCH
OF A SHARK

Peter Lerangis

**Illustrated by
Walter P. Martishius**

**A Byron Preiss
Visual Publications, Inc., Book**

Scholastic Inc.

New York Toronto London Auckland Sydney

Special thanks to Jean Feiwel, Greg Holch, Regina Griffin,
and Bruce Stevenson.

Book design by Alex Jay
Cover painting by Paul Rivoche
Cover design by Alex Jay
Mechanicals by Mary LeCleir

Editor: Ruth Ashby

THE COUNTDOWN BEGINS...

You are an explorer. You journey to places no one has ever been and face dangers no one has ever known.

Now you have a new assignment. In a moment you'll be given a briefing and will meet some of the other members of your team. At your disposal you will have the latest in scientific knowledge and technology.

Despite these advantages, at times you and your team may be exposed to extreme peril. Only the decisions you make will enable you to survive.

Are you willing to accept the risks? The choice is up to you.

───────────────────────────────

■ *When you're ready, turn the page.*

PROJECT SUMMARY

Your assignment: You will travel into the Bermuda Triangle to search for a runaway shark—in its jaws is a box containing the formula for the world's first shark repellent.

"Help! Shark!"

It's every swimmer's nightmare: The arms flail, the eyes widen, the head bobs up and down in the water for a few seconds before disappearing.

A shark attacks quietly and swiftly; its prey is often instantly killed. And no one has ever invented a way to repel it.

Until now, that is. Hidden on a Caribbean island, a team of scientists has developed the world's first foolproof shark repellent. But on their way to the U.S., near the treacherous Bermuda Triangle, the box containing the repellent was snatched away—by the jaws of an attacking shark!

If you can help the scientists find this mysterious shark thief, you will make it safer for people to enter the water.

■ *The following Personnel Dossiers and Equipment Report contain orientation material that will help you on your search for the runaway shark. If you prefer to take a helicopter flight directly to the ship to meet your team members, turn to page 1.*

PERSONNEL DOSSIERS

CAPTAIN OLIVER BOWMAN, skipper of the ship *Survivor* and well-known shark hunter

Born: October 29, 1932 Nantucket, Mass.

Educ.: Grade 10, Nantucket High School

Awards: 17 National Awards for Maritime Bravery; Honorary Doctorate at the Gulf Coast Institute of Marine Studies, 1984; International Award of Recognition for Maritime Achievement, 1982

Remarks: Captain Bowman is regarded as a crusty old salt with great intelligence, fierce honesty, and uncanny common sense. His career began when he dropped out of high school and stowed away on a whaling ship. He probably knows more about sharks than any of the world's experts, except for Dr. Carcharias.

He enjoys playing tricks on shipmates, a trait perceived as hostile by many.

PERSONNEL DOSSIERS

DR. VIVIAN TESTOUB, Marine Biochemist; inventor of MultiFreak and Chaser-Tracer Box

Born: March 26, 1952 Calcutta, India

Educ.: Ph.D., Mansfield/Barker Institute of Technology, 1979

Awards: Coleman-Mansfield Genetic Studies Fellowship, 1981; Chairmanship of the International Pelagic Conference, 1982–1985; Rubado Grant for radio technology research, 1984; Laud-Bobbs Company Award for Marine Biochemical Research, 1986

Remarks: Dr. Testoub is unique in her mastery of *two* fields: marine biology and radio technology. Her research in marine genetic engineering led to the discovery of a foolproof shark repellent (Shark Chaser) cloned from cells of the Moses sole.

She is reputed to be quiet and friendly but erratic: moods of intense concentration alternate with a dizzy forgetfulness. Dr. Carcharias is fond of her, but Captain Bowman thinks she's a flake. Her hobby is rock collecting.

PERSONNEL DOSSIERS

PROFESSOR TIBURON "TIB" CAR-CHARIAS, renowned shark expert

Born: July 7, 1949 Freeport, N.Y.

Educ.: Ph.D., Harbor Oceanographic Institute, 1975; postdoctoral work at Dunster University

Awards/Publications: Numerous scholarly articles in major marine-life and oceanographic journals; Evans Award for Pioneering Research in Shark Anatomy and Behavior, 1979; Lewis Heald Senior Professorship at the Harbor Institute; seven National Prizes for Shark Research

Remarks: Professor Carcharias is considered to be the country's leading expert on sharks. Without his partnership, Dr. Testoub might not have been able to develop her shark repellent, Shark Chaser.

He is witty and charming, and he has a reputation as something of a ladies' man. He and Captain Bowman will identify and capture sharks, while Dr. Testoub operates the MultiFreak.

EQUIPMENT REPORT

THE *SURVIVOR:* World-famous shark-tracking vessel. Over the years its crew members, headed by Captain Oliver Bowman, have captured many sharks and withstood the attacks of countless others.

SHARK CHASER: The world's first 100 percent effective shark repellent, invented by Dr. Vivian Testoub. She cloned the repellent from cells of the Moses sole, a fish that secretes a potent shark poison.

CHASER-TRACER BOX: A theft-proof container invented by Dr. Vivian Testoub for the shark repellent. The box is made of heavy-gauge metal; its lock has a computer-coded combination. It contains a device that transmits and receives radio signals.

MULTIFREAK: Nickname for Multifrequency Communicator, a device that sends out radio waves to the Chaser-Tracer Box. This stimulates the box to emit a return radio wave of the same frequency. The frequency can be adjusted to avoid jamming signals. Also invented by Dr. Testoub.

CHAIN-MAIL SHARK SUIT: A diving suit made of a puncture-proof metal alloy, used to protect against underwater shark bites.

HARPO: A computer-guided launcher that shoots harpoons attached to a tow line. It has an accuracy to .00001 inches.

UNDERWATER VIDEO WRIST MONITOR/VOICE DECODER: An electronic device with which you will be able to communicate with your team, even if you must speak underwater.

■ *End orientation material. If you want more information on the world of sharks, turn to page 110.*

■ *If you are ready to begin your assignment now, turn to page 1.*

"There it is!"

"What did you say?"

"I said, 'there it is!' I'm picking it up on my radar!" The helicopter pilot, Captain Roland "Rowe" Terblaide, is practically shouting at you. Between the wind, the thunder, and the whirring of the copter blades, you can barely hear him. "Are you sure you want to do this?" he continues. "I know *I* wouldn't!"

"Yes," you answer bravely, although a voice inside of you is screaming "NO!" You don't look forward to climbing down a rope to a small ship in this weather.

"I wish you good luck," Captain Terblaide shouts, "but I have to remind you —everything about this mission is to remain top-secret!"

"I know!" you yell back. "But I don't understand what's the big deal about a shark repellent!"

"The *big deal?* It's one of the greatest inventions of the century! All throughout history, plenty of people have tried to develop a substance that could repel sharks—but no one came up with it until Dr. Testoub invented the Shark Chaser formula! And it took her three years of steady work with her assistants on that little Caribbean island! One drop of that stuff in the water and sharks scatter for twenty miles!"

"So why not announce it to the world?" you ask.

"It has to be tested and approved first, and then patented! It's very controversial, you know—they used gene-splicing! Who knows what kind of harmful by-products may have been formed? Besides, if they announced it to the press, every crook alive would want to steal the formula! They could manufacture the stuff and make a fortune selling it on the black market!"

"It's hard to believe three top experts could *lose* something like that!"

"They didn't lose it!" Captain Terblaide protested. "They were taking it by boat to the mainland, when a shark came from nowhere and tore a hole in the hull of the ship! It happened to be the cargo hold, and the darned animal just swallowed up the box that contained the formula and the only existing specimen of the repellent!"

"That sounds fishy to me," you say.

"Of course it's fishy!" Terblaide shouts. "Most sharks are!"

"You know what I mean!"

Terblaide is grinning at his joke. "Yeah, I do. But everyone assures me the whole thing really happened!"

Through the heavy clouds below, you see the vague form of a ship—the *Survivor*. It looks long and sturdy, but the waves are tossing it around as if it were a toy. As your helicopter gets closer, you can make out three people peering up at you from the deck.

Captain Terblaide grabs a heavy brown rope that's anchored to the helicopter. He tosses it out. You watch as the rope jerks around in the wind. The end of it swings near the ship and then out over the water.

"Go ahead, pal," Captain Terblaide says. "I've done worse. When you get to the end of the rope, just don't jump until you're right over the deck of the ship! I'll be right above you the whole time!"

Some consolation, you think. Slowly you lower yourself down the slippery rope. In seconds your hair is soaking wet, and it feels as if the wind is punching you in the ears. The three people aboard the *Survivor* are carefully urging you on, but they look as scared as you are.

Soon you've reached the bottom of the rope. You're about fifteen feet from the deck of the ship. You signal up to Captain Terblaide to lower you a little more. As you descend, the wind keeps blowing you out over the water.

The *Survivor* is coming nearer, but very slowly. You clutch onto the rope, not knowing what to do. Above you, Captain Terblaide is signaling you to be calm—but his helicopter is bobbing and weaving in the wind. To your left you hear anxious voices shouting at you from the ship.

You look down at the whitecaps on the ocean. But some of them aren't whitecaps at all—they're the gleaming teeth of a huge shark, waiting for you with open jaws!

■ *If you've had enough, climb back up the rope. Turn to page 10.*

■ *Want to go on? Lift your legs and wait for the* Survivor *to pull up beside you. Turn to page 14.*

When you awaken, Dr. Testoub is still standing beside you. She seems impatient.

"Awake now?" she asks.

"I think so," you say as you shake your head, trying to force the water out of your ears.

She smiles and hands you a towel. "While you're using this, I'll start right in, if you don't mind."

"Of course n—"

"Good!" she interrupts. "Now, as you know, our island facility is very small, and manufacturing Shark Chaser is a complex process. So we were only able to produce a beakerful, after which we immediately set sail for the mainland. As a safeguard, I was able to devise a small, airtight, theft-proof metal box, into which I put the repellent and its top-secret formula."

"All of which was snatched away this morning by a shark," Prof. Carcharias continues. "And we intend to find it, with your help."

The whole mission sounds crazy to you. "You plan to find one specific shark in the entire Atlantic Ocean? How?" you ask.

"With MultiFreak!" Dr. Testoub says. She pats a portable computerized gadget that looks like some kind of high-tech radio. "Short for Multifrequency Communicator. This little thing can contact the box that contains Shark Chaser, which I call the Chaser-Tracer Box. MultiFreak sends out radio waves to a receptor on the box, which then emits a return signal of the same frequency. To avoid jamming signals, MultiFreak can adjust the frequency it sends out."

Captain Bowman has been fidgeting in a corner. He looks upset. "Ain't it a kicker, though?" he cuts in. "She designs this thing to protect against crooks, and then a *shark* ends up stealing it!"

"Yes, Captain," Dr. Testoub says icily. "But *because* of MultiFreak, we have a chance of tracking the shark down."

"Good luck in this weather," Captain Bowman retorts.

"Wait a minute," you say, "maybe the shark was *sent* by criminals to get the Shark Chaser formula."

Prof. Carcharias puffs on his pipe and chuckles. "Interesting theory, my friend," he says. "But flawed. Sharks are long on instinct but short on intelligence. It's doubtful that they can be trained like porpoises to do complicated tasks."

"You're right. I guess that doesn't really make much sense," you say.

But Dr. Testoub is lost in thought. "Don't be too sure," she says, tapping her chin.

Captain Bowman is still restless. "OK, you lazy landlubbers," he barks, "let's make ourselves useful—time to make some shark bait!"

He steps out and then returns with a pile of fish that were caught earlier. Prof. Carcharias pulls a meat grinder out from underneath a tarpaulin. Dr. Testoub looks at you and rolls her eyes. "You'll *love* this," she says.

Your three shipmates begin grinding the fish into a large mound, which they then pack into three plastic bags. The bait is pretty gruesome-looking, not to mention the stench. You start to feel sick.

Captain Bowman says, "I thought we'd be able to use these today, but looks like we've got to wait till the storm dies down, which'll probably be tomorrow. Guess we'll store it in Cabin C; I think it'll keep OK overnight."

Dr. Testoub and Prof. Carcharias look at you for a reaction. You ask Captain Bowman, "What's in Cabin C?"

"That's your sleeping quarters," he replies.

You turn green at the thought of sleeping in the same room with bags of smelly ground-up fish.

■ *You must obey the captain; maybe he's testing your courage. Turn to page 11.*

■ *No way are you going to sleep with a roomful of smelly fish. Turn to page 22.*

"AIEEEEEEE!!!!" Screaming, you rush back up the rope and into the helicopter. (Funny how you could never do that in gym class.) You huddle in the copilot's seat and fumble with the seat belt.

"Lost the old nerve, huh?" Captain Terblaide says.

"J-j-just get me out of here! Quick!" you scream.

Captain Terblaide pats you on the shoulder. Then he pulls in the rope and lifts the helicopter high into the clouds.

"OK, kid," he says. "Sit tight. We're going home."

You may be missing the adventure of a lifetime, but you'd rather be at home, safe and alive.

THE END

Walking slowly, with a sick feeling in your stomach, you take the bags of ground-up fish to your cabin. When you open the door, your worst fears come true: the room is the size of a closet. No corner to hide the fish, no bathroom.

You look around for something to cover the bags with. Outside in the hallway you see a huge metal trash can. Maybe you can put it upside down, *over* the bags. You drag the trash can into your cabin; it weighs a ton. You turn it on its side next to the fish. Then you struggle to lift the bottom end up. You just about have it up when the ship lurches in the choppy waters.

CRASH! The can comes toppling down, bringing Prof. Carcharias on the run.

One look at you sprawled on the floor with the can and your fish, and he breaks into laughter.

"Don't let Bowman know you took him seriously," he says. "He'll *never* let you forget it!"

"What do you mean?"

12

"He didn't really mean for you to sleep with those stinking bags. That's just his sense of humor."

You smile back at Prof. Carcharias, all the while feeling like a total fool. You're happy to take the bags of fish back up to the deck, but now you know to watch out for Bowman's "sense of humor."

When you get there, you notice the sun is beginning to peek through the clouds. Maybe you will be hunting today, after all. You look out toward the horizon, and your jaw drops.

Slicing through the water toward the boat are a group of dark, triangular fins —the unmistakable sign of sharks.

■ *You scream a warning to your shipmates. Turn to page 18.*

The shark's jaws clamp shut just inches below your feet, which you've pulled as high up as you can. But you don't know how long you can hang here. Your hands are getting tired, the rope is slippery—and the shark is still circling below!

It sounds like the wind is picking up, until you realize you're hearing the sound of a straining motor. You turn and see the *Survivor* approaching.

"Hang on a couple more seconds!" the ship captain shouts. "We're almost there!"

Heaving upward on waves and then slapping down onto the water below, the *Survivor* pulls up beside you, just as your fingers are about to slide off.

"In you go," the captain says as he grabs you around the waist and pulls you aboard the ship. "Didn't your mama teach you not to go out in the rain?"

Bowman is a beefy man with leathery skin. His gray beard has flecks of red in it, and his hands are the size of seat cushions. He winks at you and motions everyone to follow him into the ship's cabin.

Inside it smells musty and feels warm. Your knees buckle and you sit on a bench. You look around. The cabin is paneled in blond knotty wood, covered by nautical charts, maps, and color drawings of sharks with Latin names below them. You take off your foul-weather gear and drop it on the floor. Then you check your backpack. Everything is still there: pens, an underwater camera, a pocket lighter, a compass, and a knife.

"I'm Captain Oliver Bowman," the gray-haired man says. "Welcome to the *Survivor*. Hope you don't expect a comfy trip —we're going to be near the Bermuda Triangle. You'll probably be spending time thrashing around in the water, so put this on." He gives you something that looks like a little TV on a wristband. "It's an underwater video wrist monitor and voice decoder. In plain English, that means you'll be able to see and talk to any of us, even if you have to speak underwater."

Then he points to a quiet, dark-skinned woman in a lab coat. "That's Dr. Vivian Testoub, a biochemist and electronics expert who developed Shark Chaser—a nice gal, but I'd like her better if she didn't insist on bringing her rock collection with her." Dr. Testoub looks annoyed as Bowman indicates the other man. "And this guy's name I can never pronounce . . ."

"Professor Tiburon Carcharias—Tib to my friends," says the man. Adjusting his green tweed coat, he sits on a chair opposite you and lights up a pipe. His thin mustache and dark hair remind you of Robin Hood. "That was an adventure of equal parts bravery and recklessness! Just what we need for this mission."

"Now then," Dr. Testoub says, "are you ready to begin your briefing?"

You nod your head—and then promptly fall asleep from exhaustion.

■ *Wake up an hour later. Turn to page 6.*

"Sharks! Sharks!" you shout at the top of your lungs. The trio comes running to the stern, led by Captain Bowman.

Bowman looks over the railing and shakes his head. "Calm the kid down, will ya, Tib?" he says, turning to walk away.

You protest, "But—but—I saw their fins! There was a whole pack of them!"

"There's a whole pack, all right," Prof. Carcharias says, looking over the railing. You hear strange squeaking noises and glance down.

It's a family of friendly porpoises!

"Sharks aren't the only animals that have dorsal fins," Prof. Carcharias says.

You're a little embarrassed, but you feel concerned about the chirping creatures. "They must be so helpless; the ocean is dangerous!" you say.

"Don't forget, they're mammals," Prof. Carcharias says. "They're highly intelligent fighters. When sharks travel in groups, each one attacks on his own. But porpoises—"

A loud squeal cuts Prof. Carcharias off. A few yards away from the porpoises, a shark is moving in for the kill.

Within minutes, you see what Prof. Carcharias is talking about. The porpoises scurry about for a while and then form a circle around the shark. They look like Indians around a covered wagon. The shark lunges at a porpoise. But as soon as he does, another porpoise uses his bottlenose to butt the shark in the gills. One by one, the porpoises distract the shark's attention. And each time it happens, another porpoise hits the shark. Before long, the porpoises have the shark rolling end over end. And soon the shark just stops moving, and its lifeless form sinks to the bottom.

"Incredible!" you say. "But the shark *sank* after it died. Shouldn't it have floated to the top?"

"Good point. Sharks have no air bladders, so if they stop swimming they sink. Some of them can rest on the ocean floor, but most can't—they have to keep swimming their whole lives! In fact, a shark was once tagged in Massachusetts and recaptured in the West Indies four months later. It had swum 2,700 miles—an average of twenty-two and a half miles a day, *every day for four months!*"

"Really? Then when do they sleep?"

"We don't know. It's thought—"

Your conversation is then interrupted by a loud beeping noise. "It's MultiFreak!" he says. You both run to the bow of the ship, where Dr. Testoub is operating MultiFreak. Way off on the horizon you see a huge, dark shape in the water. This must be it.

Captain Bowman is aiming Harpo, a computer-guided harpoon launcher. Harpo can fire with an accuracy to .00001 inches, and its harpoon is attached to 500 yards of super-strong nylon rope, so that the prey can be pulled in. "Identify this beast with the binoculars, somebody!" he shouts.

"Do you really think that's necessary? We have the signal!" answers Dr. Testoub.

■ *Dr. Testoub is right; forget the binoculars and lure the creature closer by throwing the bait overboard. Turn to page 32.*

■ *Grab the binoculars. Turn to page 24.*

You leave the cabin and take the bags down through the hatch to your sleeping quarters. When you get to your cabin door, you look down the hallway and notice another hatch that must lead to the stern of the ship.

Quietly you climb up through the hatch with the bags. Sure enough, you come out onto the stern. Your shipmates are nowhere to be seen. You spot a long rope lying on the deck, which you tie to the three bags. Then you tie the other end of the rope to the ship's railing and toss the bags overboard.

No one will notice that the ship is towing the bait, you figure. Tomorrow morning you can get up earlier than everyone, pull the bags in, and bring them back to your room!

But just then you realize your clever little plan may not even be necessary. The sun has started breaking through the clouds—it looks like you may be using the bait today!

You'll have to give the bait to Captain Bowman, so you begin to pull it in. You look left and right over your shoulder, hoping you won't be caught. As the bags come to the surface of the water, you reach down to lift them up.

At the same time, a dark form leaps out of the water at your hand. In the water are a half dozen black, sickle-shaped fins.

■ *You throw the bags on the deck and scream for help. Turn to page 18.*

"I've got them!" you say as you grab the binoculars. You peer through them at the dark creature.

"Looks like a big one!" Captain Bowman shouts.

He's right; this one is much too big to be a porpoise. It's got to be a shark. You follow its movements, hoping it will break through the surface of the water. It disappears over the horizon line, and then comes back. Then it dives downward and out of sight.

"I've lost it!" Captain Bowman says. "What do you see?"

"Nothing now! But I'll keep looking!" you answer.

For a few minutes the creature is nowhere in sight. Then the water darkens again and the huge creature comes to the surface. A triangular dorsal fin cuts through the water.

"We've got the signal strong on MultiFreak," Dr. Testoub says.

This time you don't want it to get away.

Immediately you shout, "Fire!" As Captain Bowman aims Harpo, you notice something strange through the binoculars. A water spray comes shooting out of the creature—maybe it's not a shark after all. It must be a *whale* that swallowed the Chaser-Tracer Box!

■ *You're close to the goal of your mission; let Captain Bowman shoot. Turn to page 39.*

■ *Shout for Captain Bowman to stop; you can't bear for him to shoot a whale. Turn to page 28.*

"I hate to do this, buddies, but you give me no choice," says Captain Bowman as he aims Harpo.

The whales are getting nearer, and you have no idea how Bowman can possibly harpoon them all. With dread you realize he doesn't seem to want to shoot.

"Please, Captain!" you shout. "It's them or us!"

"Not necessarily," Captain Bowman replies. He backs away from Harpo and watches. The whales are now forming a circle around a large, dark object, which rises to the surface—and spouts into the air. It's another whale! You see its mouth open, revealing what looks like a huge white sheet of teeth.

"They're attacking that toothy whale!" you say.

"Those aren't teeth," Captain Bowman says, shaking his head. "They're baleen plates. They're like big filters. This kind of whale opens his mouth and lets water rush in. But he doesn't swallow the water.

His tongue pushes it back out through the plates."

"What good is that?" you ask.

"Well, the plates trap tons of small animals called krill, which are like shrimp. That's all the baleen whales eat."

"But the killer whales have teeth, don't they?"

Your question is answered before your eyes. The killer whales have surrounded the baleen whale and are biting into his skin.

"Poor guy doesn't have a chance," Captain Bowman says.

All four of you turn away from this gruesome sight.

"Hang on," says Captain Bowman. "I'm setting a course away from these critters —and *fast*, just in case they get ideas about us!"

■ *Turn to page 41.*

There's got to be another way to get Shark Chaser without killing the whale. Captain Bowman is about to fire. As loud as you can, you shout, *"Stop! Don't shoot!"*

Just in time. You've distracted Captain Bowman, and he looks annoyed. Then, large enough to see with the naked eye, a geyser of water shoots skyward from the whale, as if in thanks.

Your three shipmates breathe a sigh of relief as they realize why you stopped Captain Bowman. Bowman claps you on the back and says, "You know, kid, at first I thought you were a flake. But you just prevented me from helping wipe out an endangered species!"

"But don't you want to get Shark Chaser back?" you ask. "The whale must have the Chaser-Tracer Box!"

Dr. Testoub answers, "No, the damage to the hull was definitely done by a shark. This whale fooled us. You see, sometimes whales are tagged with radio transmitters

so scientists can study their migration patterns. That's what MultiFreak picked up."

Together you watch as the whale is joined by about ten others. One of them jumps clear out of the water. Its jet-black body gleams in the sun, and you notice its belly is white.

"They're killer whales," says Dr. Testoub. "You can tell by the body color. Also, they travel in packs, led by a male, which we call a bull. The one we avoided was probably the leader."

"And you can tell that because we saw him before we saw the others, right?" you ask.

"Right! He traveled ahead of the rest. And I can also tell he's a full-grown male because the dorsal fin is curved at the tip."

While Dr. Testoub is talking, you notice something strange about the way the whales are moving.

"Um, Dr. Testoub," you ask, "do killer whales attack in groups, like the porpoises that attacked the shark?"

"Yes, killer whales are related to porpoises! You have uncanny powers of observation!"

"Not so uncanny," you say with a gulp. "What else can they be doing?" You point out to sea.

Both of you turn pale as you see the entire pack of killer whales speeding toward the *Survivor*.

■ *Now's the time for Captain Bowman to use Harpo.* Turn to page 26.

■ *Hang tight as Captain Bowman moves away from the whales as fast as possible.* Turn to page 41.

You're determined to be the hero this time. Prof. Carcharias reaches for the binoculars, but you have a better idea. You run for the three bags of ground fish. You can use them to lure the shark closer to the ship. Then it'll be much easier for Captain Bowman to harpoon the shark.

You hear Captain Bowman's voice saying, "I'm locked on target, Tib! Do I have a confirmation?"

"One second, Captain," Prof. Carcharias says, adjusting the binoculars.

You grab the bait and drop it into the water, hoping the shark will smell it from way out there. You remember reading that a shark can smell fish oils in the water up to a quarter mile away. Quickly you let out slack on the rope, keeping your eye on the distant shape.

Just then Prof. Carcharias's voice cuts through the air: *"Hold your fire! It's not a shark! It's a whale! It's a whale!"*

Sure enough, a plume of water comes spraying out of the animal. Captain Bowman lets go of Harpo and mops his brow in relief.

You start to pull in the bait, but it's too late. At that moment, a ferocious tiger shark jumps out of the water. Its jaws clamp on to the rope. Before you can let go, you're yanked into the sea. The porpoises are nowhere to be seen, and you become a very tasty gourmet lunch.

THE END

You swim as fast as you can to the surface. You remember being told that the batlike fish is called a manta, and it's not harmful. But you're not sure about some of those other lurking things.

You take a last look down and discover your fears have come true. The thing you noticed hidden on the ocean floor is a shark, and it's coming right for you! You realize it's a nurse shark, the type that rests at the bottom of the sea, puffing its gills in and out.

Just as you're about to break to the surface, the nurse shark bites into your flipper. It shakes its head back and forth, ripping a piece loose. You look down to see your toes peeking through—all five of them. The shark won't let go; it's trying to drag you down. You shake off your flipper, and your foot is free. It looks like you got away with only a scratch.

You dart back up to the *Survivor* and hop on deck, pleased at your narrow escape. Fortunately, there's no one in sight.

You sneak toward the main cabin to take off the scuba suit. You don't know how you're going to explain the missing flipper.

When you're halfway across the deck, you hear a loud clanking noise. You spin around. The door to the other hatch crashes open, and out of it steps a stiff-walking knight in chain mail!

■ *Are you hallucinating? Turn to page 45.*

36

You sneak into the main cabin. There you find Captain Bowman's scuba gear. You take it back to the deck and put it on. Then you grab a flashlight from your backpack and plunge into the water.

You're amazed at what's around you. To your left, the coral is thick with twisted markings, like an enormous, yellow brain. Below you is a pinkish coral formation that looks like a maze whose walls are sticking straight up at you. Just beyond that there's white coral that looks like hundreds of long, fuzzy fingers.

In your initial briefing for this mission, you were told about coral reef: it's formed by tiny animals called polyps. They're shaped like tubes, and their bodies are covered with hard, spiny skeletons. These polyps attach to a solid surface underwater and then they secrete lime, which becomes a kind of cement. Over time, thousands of polyps attach themselves to the lime. As the polyps multiply and others attach on, the reef grows. So the massive motionless coral isn't rock. It's actually teeming with life!

You're amazed at the strange beauty down here. Wedged into the coral are giant blue and pink clams, and sea anemones that have green and white tentacles. Strange little spotted fish suddenly puff up like balloons when you come near. Seahorses poke their snouts among the blades of sea grass, and one of those blades moves away—it's actually a thin pipefish! And a bright-green fish spreads its fins like wings and swims away between the long, black spines of a sea urchin. You notice a big-eyed striped fish, swimming peacefully through the openings in the reef. It wanders near the rock you wanted to bring back—and suddenly disappears into it. The "rock" has a mouth!

It's not a rock at all—it's a stonefish. It hangs out at the bottom of the ocean, waiting for unsuspecting prey. On its surface are spines that are poisonous to the touch. Some surprise that would have made for Dr. Testoub!

You sigh with relief. This dive is fascinating but creepy. You want to go back up, but you have a feeling you're being watched.

Looking around, you notice a large creature lurking on the ocean floor and hidden by coral. At the same time, a dark shadow passes over you. You shoot your eyes up to see a huge creature glide above your head. It looks like a flying bat—but it's about twenty feet across!

■ *Get out of here right away; swim up to the* Survivor. *Turn to page 34.*

■ *Stay still until you feel safe. Turn to page 47.*

When Captain Bowman notices the spouting water, he tries to pull back. But it's too late. Harpo makes a dead-on hit.

Your shipmates' faces turn pale as they stare at the injured beast, which flails in the water and then sinks out of sight. "It's a whale," Dr. Testoub mutters in quiet shock.

"Brilliant deduction," Captain Bowman snaps back. You can feel his temper rising as he turns to look at you. "You were in an awful hurry to give me the *Fire* signal, weren't you?" he says. "We just brought an endangered species closer to extinction! That's the whole reason I asked you to identify our target first!"

He storms away into the cabin, followed by Prof. Carcharias. You feel awful. You say to Dr. Testoub, "But we need to get Shark Chaser back, don't we? I thought I was doing the right thing."

Dr. Testoub sighs. "We were concerned that this kind of thing might happen. You see, often whales are tagged with radio transmitters so scientists can study their migration patterns. That's what Multi-Freak picked up. Next time remember to wait until you see the creature, OK?"

You hear a voice behind you. "I'm afraid there's not going to be a next time." It's Prof. Carcharias, walking grimly toward you. He continues, "Captain Bowman is calling the mainland. He's taking you off the project. Nothing I said could stop him. I'm awfully sorry."

You realize there's no room for mistakes on this journey. You pack up your belongings and prepare for the trip home.

THE END

Captain Bowman steers sharply away, and the *Survivor* cuts through the water faster than you thought possible. In the distance, the killer whales have surrounded another prey, but you can't tell what it is.

Relieved, Dr. Testoub excuses herself to make a call on a mobile telephone she takes from her lab coat pocket. You pretend to watch Captain Bowman as he resets his course. But you really want to listen to Dr. Testoub's conversation. You stroll closer to her as she begins to speak.

"Hello, CORD headquarters, please. Elliot? It's Testoub. Report crossed signal with tagged cetacean at the following coordinates. . . . What? . . . Are you kidding? . . . Why? . . . How can you be in such a hurry after all this time? Give me two weeks. . . . Look, I'll talk to you later!"

Dr. Testoub flicks off the phone and begins pacing angrily.

"I couldn't help but overhear," you say. "What's CORD?"

"Corporation for Oceanic Research and

Development. They make underwater research equipment—submarines, cameras, robotic devices. And they've funded this whole project from the start." She slaps her hand on the railing. "And now that arrogant, twerpy new director, Elliot Brine, wants us to give up the search!"

"But his company will make a fortune on Shark Chaser," you say. "Not to mention how many lives will be saved!"

"No kidding! But now that we've lost it, he says it's a waste of money to search for it. He wants us to come right home, but I told him no way!"

Soon the *Survivor* stops as Captain Bowman does some minor engine repairs. You and Dr. Testoub wander over to the railing. She's sulking about her conversation.

You both look out at the crystal-clear water. The ship is over an unusually shallow area, and you can see strange-colored coral formations below.

"I'm dying to go scuba diving!" you say.

"So am I," Dr. Testoub replies, distracted from her anger. "I could certainly add to my rock collection here."

"You think Captain Bowman would allow us?" you ask.

Dr. Testoub frowns. "Frankly, I'm tired of *that* man's arrogance, too. Maybe he should discover a hobby of his own; it might sweeten his personality."

With that, she walks away, muttering about Bowman and Elliot Brine. You remember Bowman's snide remarks about her rock collection. Looking down, you see a small, unusual-looking rock. It's clear Dr. Testoub needs cheering up. Maybe you should get her that rock.

■ *Dive down to get it. Turn to page 36.*

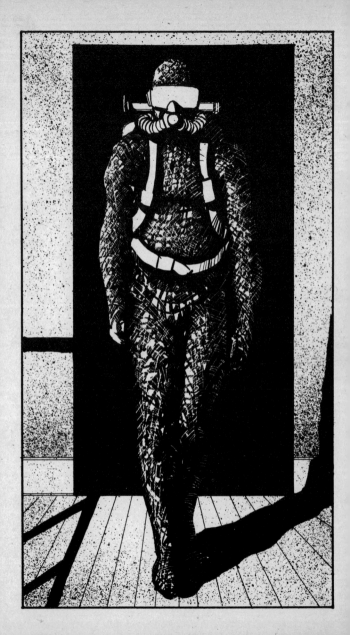

You must be seeing things; maybe it's sunstroke. The armored knight approaches with slow strides. You back away cautiously—right into the three bags of shark bait! The bags burst open as you plop right down on them.

From the open hatch behind the knight you hear explosive laughter. It's Prof. Carcharias; he's been watching this whole episode. The knight takes off his helmet, revealing Captain Bowman's grinning face.

"Scared you, huh? How do you like our metal diving suit? Wear this baby underwater and any shark that bites you will have a huge dentist bill!"

You're getting to like Bowman's sense of humor less and less. His "jokes" always seem to leave you smelling like fish.

You stand up, force a smile, and say, "That suit's amazing! Have you tested it?"

"Sure have," he replies as he takes the suit off. "It's made of a special metal alloy that can withstand the bite of all but the biggest sharks. At some point we'll have to use it."

"Maybe sooner than expected," Prof. Carcharias says.

With a loud *whirrrr*, the reel on Captain Bowman's stationary rod is being violently pulled out to sea.

"We got one!" Captain Bowman yells.

It takes a half hour of fighting, but he manages to pull in a seven-foot-long hammerhead shark that has strands of thick netting embedded in its skin. You're fascinated by its weird eyes on either side of its long, horizontal head.

"It's a small one," says Bowman. "They grow up to fifteen feet. Let's pull it in."

He attaches the line to a crane that's bolted to the deck and pulls the hammerhead alongside the boat.

"What's all that rope sticking out of its skin?" you ask.

"It's the reason he was so easy to catch," Bowman says. "You see, sometimes sharks swim into tuna-fishing nets. And they can't swim backward, so they get stuck. This one managed to get away, but he's pretty weak." He turns to Prof. Carcharias. "Tib, why don't you get me a shotgun, so I can put him out of his misery while we drag him along."

But that won't be necessary. At that moment another shark leaps out of the water and takes a hefty bite out of the hammerhead's side!

■ *Turn to page 51.*

You watch silently as the shadow passes. You recognize it as a manta. Although frightening-looking, you know it's harmless to humans. But you're not sure about what's lurking on the ocean floor behind the coral. Slowly you move away from that unseen creature. You hold onto the edges of the coral with your left hand, which is still clutching your flashlight.

Clank! Something's got a hold on your flashlight. You pull on it, at the same time flicking on the light.

You gasp in terror. Clutching onto the flashlight with sharp teeth is a moray eel, hiding inside a coral crevice. Its face is brown, lizardlike, and *very* determined to have your flashlight.

Much more so than you are. You quickly let go of the flashlight and swim up to the *Survivor*.

On board, you plop down on the deck in relief. You're lucky to have escaped to a safe place. At least you think so—until you hear a rhythmic clanking noise followed by a loud slam. You spin around to see a strange apparition rise from one of the hatches—a knight dressed in full-body chain mail!

■ *Turn to page 45.*

No one is around to see you. You hop into the armored suit and attach the helmet so that every inch of your body is covered.

With a mixture of excitement and fear, you approach the hammerhead. It sees you. You slowly reach out your arm. It bares its enormous white teeth. Maybe this isn't such a great idea, you think.

But it's too late. The hammerhead clamps its jaw down around your arm with as much strength as it can muster.

You cringe and then look down, expecting to see a bloody stump. But your entire arm is intact. In fact, as you pull it out you notice that a few of the hammerhead's teeth have broken off. Where the teeth were, you see rows of replacement teeth waiting to grow in. Including those teeth, there are hundreds in the shark's mouth! You've heard that a shark replaces its own teeth about every eight years, but you never thought you'd see first-hand evidence!

Just then your arm starts to throb. The bite may not have penetrated, but you sure felt the pressure! You take off your suit and examine the huge red mark on your arm—you'd hate to have tested the suit with a full-strength shark! The hammerhead is now dead-still. That bite seems to have used up its last ounce of energy.

■ Cut the dead hammerhead loose and join Captain Bowman at the helm. *Turn to page 60.*

■ Go over to examine the hammerhead one last time before cutting it loose. *Turn to page 53.*

You turn your head away from this gruesome sight. "They actually eat each other?" you ask.

"Yep, they're real cannibals," Captain Bowman replies. "They have no mercy for *anything* when they're hungry. Especially a fellow shark who's injured."

The hammerhead jerks meekly on the line a couple of times and then stops moving.

"I think we ought to cut it loose, Oliver," Prof. Carcharias says.

"OK. Might as well give it a burial at sea," Captain Bowman says, reaching into a metal chest. He pulls out a knife the size of a machete and hands it to you. "I'll let you do the honors," he says. The two men walk off toward the helm.

You wonder if the hammerhead is really dead. You lunge toward it with the knife, to see if it flinches. But it just hangs motionlessly, jaws wide open. You look at its teeth and wonder if the chain-mail suit really would protect against a shark bite. It doesn't seem likely.

You lift the knife toward the taut fishing line. All of a sudden the hammerhead snaps its jaws. There's still some life left in it.

■ Now's your chance to test the chain-mail suit—put it on and let the shark bite your arm! Turn to page 49.

■ Quick, cut the rope and get out of the way before the shark does any damage. Turn to page 60.

That strange horizontal head still fascinates you. It looks like a long, flat loaf of bread with eyes at each end. You've read that it's one of the great mysteries of nature. You wonder if it's soft or hard. You want to touch it, but first you test if the shark is still alive. You pretend to strike its eye. It doesn't blink. But you've seen this trick before. You pick up a long pole and poke the tip of it into the hammerhead's mouth. It still doesn't budge.

Somehow, you're not convinced yet. But then you catch a glimpse of its missing midsection. It looks as if half its body has been eaten. By now this thing has got to be dead as a doornail. You reach out to touch its head.

Surprise! The hammerhead, like all sharks, is an expert at playing dead. It thrusts its open jaws at you. You can't tear your arm away—but the hammerhead can! It clamps down, pleased not to taste metal again.

The last thing you remember hearing is Dr. Testoub yelling to Captain Bowman to radio for medical help; you're going to be taken to the mainland. The project will have to go on without you.

THE END

You let go of the ship and start to swim around it. As soon as the shark sees you moving, it picks up speed and opens its mouth. Dozens of razor-sharp teeth, three inches long, flash in the sunlight.

You've never swum faster in your life. Clambering onto the jutting rock, you can feel the shark's breath as its jaws slam shut—inches short of your foot. You plant yourself firmly at the top and look down. The great white shark circles around, disappointed in losing its dinner.

You let out a nervous whoop of relief. Now your shipmates can rescue you. You turn to wave at the ship.

And what you see makes your mouth drop open.

The *Survivor* is sinking out of sight. In trying to maneuver around to get you, the ship has smashed into a sharp rock. Water is rushing into a wide gash in the hull.

The ocean stretches to the horizon in all directions. Below you, the great white shark is still circling. All you can do is wait and hope.

THE END

Suddenly the sky turns shades of purple, red, and gray. The wind sounds like a chorus of coyotes. The *Survivor* starts spinning. This was probably not the right choice.

Captain Bowman yanks the wheel to the left and right. But soon he loses control. The wheel seems to take on a life of its own; it spins in one direction, then the other.

"Stay the course! Stay the course!" Dr. Testoub cries out.

"What course?" yells Captain Bowman. "I don't know where we're going!"

The four of you are then thrown out of the helm and up against the railing. At once you notice the water looks pitch black. In the distance, waves are swelling up and rolling toward you.

You think you hear thunderous laughing as a whirlpool the size of a baseball field opens up. You feel the *Survivor* straighten out and then tilt sideways.

And in seconds your ship is swallowed up by the Bermuda Triangle.

THE END

Captain Bowman agrees to steer the *Survivor* north alongside the serpent. As you pull up to it, you see that it's not a long serpent at all. It's a school of gigantic sharks, each about forty feet long—and they're swimming in a straight line, practically nose-to-tail! With their backs and fins pulsing out of the water, they look like one long creature.

Prof. Carcharias nods his head in recognition. "Just as I thought," he says. "These clever fish have been deluding people through the ages. They're basking sharks, a rather sluggish species who travel around in these peculiar, tight schools. Nothing to fear. Like many whales, they only eat plankton."

After the school passes by, Dr. Testoub joins the two of you. In her hand is a solid metal object shaped like an Indian arrowhead.

"Does this belong to either of you?" she asks. You both shake your heads. "This is very disturbing," she continues. "I just found this in the cargo hold, and I'm almost positive it wasn't there before the shark attack."

"I imagine it's a component that fell out of some mechanical device in there, Vivian," Prof. Carcharias offers.

"Mm. Maybe you're right," she says. But she looks preoccupied with the object as she walks away.

You and Prof. Carcharias turn back to the sea and notice a long line of ominous-looking rocks just to the south of you. They stretch far in front of you, where they curve northward into the area of the Bermuda Triangle. You may be able to get around the southern end of the rocks if you cut hard, but the current is strong and chances are you'll be dashed against them.

Or else you can stay your course and take the northern route around the rocks. But you'll have to pass into the Bermuda Triangle again!

Either way is taking a big chance. What should Captain Bowman do?

■ *Head north to make sure you avoid the rocks. Turn to page 62.*

■ *Head south to avoid the Bermuda Triangle. Turn to page 67.*

The sun is setting and Captain Bowman is in a story-telling mood. It seems as if he's going to describe every shark he's ever had to capture. You start to doze at about the fifteenth one. You excuse yourself, shower off the smell of the fish you landed on, wash your clothes, and settle into your sleeping quarters for an early sleep.

You wake up with a start the next morning. The boat is rocking up and down again. You dress, sling your backpack over your shoulders, and run up to the helm. All three of your shipmates are there. Captain Bowman is struggling with the instrument board. The compass is spinning wildly.

"Hang on!" says Captain Bowman when he sees you. "Ever heard of the Bermuda Triangle? Well, here it is!"

You reach into your backpack for your compass, but it's doing the same thing.

"What's going to happen?" you ask.

Prof. Carcharias looks scared. "They say

ships lose their bearings and get sucked in. But I've always thought it was just a myth!"

"Well, your guess is as good as mine," says Captain Bowman. "I have no idea where to go. Got any suggestions, kid?" he asks you.

■ *Tell him to steer right. Turn to page 56.*

■ *Tell him to steer left. Turn to page 65.*

A turn south looks like certain death; Captain Bowman stays the course and heads for the northernmost rock.

You and your shipmates are tight-lipped. You're now entering the area you barely escaped not long ago. As before, the compass starts gyrating wildly. You look for the sky to change, for the water to open up. You hear rumblings in the distance. The water becomes a little choppy.

"Are you sure this is the correct course, Captain?" Dr. Testoub asks. You can see that her teeth are chattering.

"That's what I'm hoping!" Captain Bowman answers, with an edge to his voice. "But I wouldn't bet your rock collection on it!"

It doesn't look promising. But as you approach the northern tip of the rocks, the skies are bright and the water is calm.

"We're swinging around the top now!" Captain Bowman says. You breathe a sigh of relief. Dr. Testoub and Prof. Carcharias smile at you, and you all hug each other.

The four of you look on confidently as the *Survivor* makes the turn around the last, tall rock—and right into a hidden whirlpool the size of a baseball stadium!

You spin swiftly down, another mysterious casualty of the Bermuda Triangle.

THE END

All of a sudden the sky darkens. There is a moment of dead silence, and then the wind starts howling like a pack of wolves. The *Survivor* is tossed violently on the choppy ocean, which now looks black.

"Looks like we went the wrong way!" shouts Captain Bowman. "Be prepared for *anything* to happen in the Bermuda Triangle!"

Dr. Testoub and Prof. Carcharias have become so pale with fright, their faces practically glow against the black sky. You grab hands with them both as a huge wave crashes over the ship.

But just when you're sure the *Survivor* isn't going to make it, Bowman's compass springs to life and the sea calms down. He carefully checks his instruments, and his face breaks into a broad grin.

"Guess what, mates?" he says. "We were just skirting the Triangle. It should be clear sailing from here out!"

All four of you cheer as the stormy sky

gives way to sun. Prof. Carcharias dances a jig, and Captain Bowman and Dr. Testoub smile at each other for the first time on this trip.

But then everything comes to a sudden stop as you all catch a glimpse of something strange in the ocean.

Maybe you *are* in the Bermuda Triangle after all. Swimming slowly toward the ship is a sea serpent two hundred feet long, with half a dozen dorsal fins!

■ *Have Captain Bowman steer toward it so you can study it. Turn to page 58.*

■ *Avoid the serpent. Turn to page 88.*

The *Survivor* vibrates as it scrapes against a massive underwater rock formation.

"I don't know if we can make it!" Captain Bowman says. He cuts the *Survivor* as hard south as he can to avoid the huge chain of rocks that rises out of the ocean. The ship's motor groans with the strain. You can't tell if you'll make it around the southernmost rock. It looks awfully close . . .

CRRRUNCH! With a deafening metallic noise, the entire starboard side of the *Survivor* is lifted out of the water as it sideswipes the rock.

"Everyone grab hold of something!" Captain Bowman shouts. He hangs on to his steering wheel, and you and Dr. Testoub grab a railing. But Prof. Carcharias has lost his balance. With a yelp and a clatter, he slides down the slanted deck and into the sea.

You hear him thrashing in the water. "Somebody help me!" he cries. "I—I—don't know how to swim!"

You dive in after him—clothes, back-pack, and all. The current is carrying him away from the ship and he's in a panic. You try to grab onto him, but you can't. His arms are flailing wildly and each time you get close they bat you away. You see his head pop in and out of the water three times. Finally you're able to wrap your arm around his chest.

"Be still!" you shout. "I've got you!" He calms down a little and you swim him toward the ship.

"This is embarrassing. I'm afraid I've gained all of my marine expertise on dry land," he says, reaching for a port railing that's slanting down over the water.

"No sweat, your secret's safe with me," you reply.

The *Survivor* keeps scraping over the rock. But at the moment Prof. Carcharias clutches the railing, the other side of the ship plops back down into the water. And the port railing lifts back up to even keel, taking Prof. Carcharias with it.

You're left facing a smooth hull with nothing to grab onto. Prof. Carcharias dangles in the air above you and shouts for help. The smiling faces of Captain Bowman and Dr. Testoub appear over the railing.

"Well, if it isn't our gold medal winner in the dog paddle!" says Bowman as he hoists Carcharias aboard. "We made it, Tib!"

"Hey, what about me?" you shout from below. But the other three are too busy congratulating each other for making it past the rock.

And behind you, closer than you'd like to admit, is a charging great white shark, the most dangerous shark known! Your life rushes before you as you realize it's too late for yelling to do any good.

■ *Swim over to the rocks and climb onto them to escape the vicious shark. Turn to page 55.*

■ *Stay still in the water. Turn to page 77.*

"I think we should drop bait and move closer," you say. "Maybe the shark's having a hunger attack ... you know, a—"

"You mean a feeding frenzy," says Prof. Carcharias. "That's very likely. Many sharks do exhibit this kind of excited behavior when they sense food."

"Good thinking, kid," Captain Bowman says to you. "Go ahead; let's get him to come to us."

You tie up some bags of bait that Bowman caught this morning, fasten them to the ship, and then toss them overboard. Meanwhile, Bowman motors closer to the crazed porbeagle.

Despite the "feeding frenzy," it doesn't seem to notice your bait. You wait about ten minutes. By now it should be chomping away at the fish. But it just continues jumping around in all directions.

"Could it be a temper tantrum?" you say.

"Maybe he's still mad they didn't cast

him in *Jaws,*" Captain Bowman suggests.

"Listen!" shouts Dr. Testoub. She fiddles with a lever on MultiFreak so that it makes rising and falling sounds. "Now look at the shark," she says.

Your eyes widen as you see what Dr. Testoub is talking about: The shark is jumping up and down with the same rhythm as MultiFreak's sounds!

"I'm going to pull us closer," says Captain Bowman.

You reach for the binoculars and look through them. As the *Survivor* approaches the shark, you notice something strange about the shark's skin. It has perfect little circles all over it.

"Is this normal for a porbeagle?" you ask Prof. Carcharias, handing him the binoculars. "Looks like it has acne scars."

He puts the binoculars up to his eyes and squints through them for a long time. "I don't believe it," he says under his breath. "Those aren't acne scars. They're *rivets!*"

Then he drops the binoculars, swings around, and shouts out, "We've got ourselves an imposter! This thing isn't a real shark at all! It's a metal robot!"

"I thought so!" yells Dr. Testoub. "Wahoooo!" You've never seen her this excited. She starts making all kinds of adjustments on MultiFreak. Her hands skillfully fly over the controls. The robot shark's jerky movements become smaller, but it still seems to be fighting, trying to break away.

"Look! Dr. Testoub is controlling its behavior!" you shout to the two men.

"Hold on to it, Vivian!" Prof. Carcharias says, rushing to her side.

"I'm trying to," she says, struggling with the switches. "But so is someone else! Quick, try to get the shark while I still have it in my control!"

"Maybe we should use Harpo," suggests Prof. Carcharias.

"I'll give it a shot," Captain Bowman answers, "but I'd hate to waste one of these harpoons . . ."

He loads Harpo and takes aim. But it's tough to get the flailing robot in the viewfinder. Finally he shouts, "Fire one!"

With a *whoosh*, the harpoon slices harmlessly into the water.

Bowman is angry now. "I can't hit this thing!" he says.

"Yes, you can," Dr. Testoub cries out. "I'm calming it down now!"

"I'll try the net," Bowman replies. He throws out a sturdy fishing net into the robot's path, but the shark easily rips it to shreds.

"Anybody have another bright idea?" he asks.

"We could try to wait for its mouth to

open and aim the harpoon inside," you say. "Then it might hook onto something in there and we can pull it in."

Captain Bowman shakes his head. "Don't know if that's the best idea. These harpoons are expensive, you know . . ."

Dr. Testoub flies into a rage when she hears this. "How can you think of that now?" she says to Captain Bowman. "You better come up with *some* way to catch that thing, Sinbad, or you'll be fishing up unemployment checks next week!"

■ *Should you try the harpoon idea? Turn to page 103.*

■ *Should you put on the chain-mail suit and go after it yourself? Turn to page 99.*

Even though it goes against your instincts, you stay as still as possible in the water. After all, sharks are more attracted to moving targets; their hearing can sense the slightest movement in water. And this one looks like it can swim much faster than you, anyway.

It is the biggest, most fearsome thing you've ever seen. It swims slowly toward you, moving side-to-side so that each eye can size you up and each nostril can smell you. Your eyes widen when you see its full length of about thirty feet.

You start to shiver with fear. The great white shark pushes its snout toward you. Then, abruptly, as if you were a pile of overcooked lima beans, it pulls its head away and turns to leave.

You have an urge to scream with relief. But it's not over yet. You are whapped across your already-bruised arm by the side of the shark. The pain is unbearable —the shark's skin feels as if it's covered with little blades. You hold in your voice, but your arm is starting to bleed.

The shark swims around in a circle. Now it seems to smell something more appetizing. Blood. It comes back for a second look, this time with its jaws wide open.

For a split second dozens of gleaming white teeth flash in the sunlight, each one of them two or three inches long. And that's the last thing you see as the shark swallows you whole!

■ *Turn to page 96.*

Everyone is beaming as you're hoisted over the railing. Prof. Carcharias pumps your hand, Captain Bowman gives you a big bear hug, and Dr. Testoub kisses you on both cheeks. You're a little embarrassed; having just been in a shark's stomach, you're not exactly fresh-smelling.

"We thought we'd never see you again," says Dr. Testoub.

"Ah, it was nothing, really," you say. "A little vacation down the alimentary canal!" *Alimentary canal* is a term you've heard that means digestive tract.

"I beg your pardon?" says Prof. Carcharias, grinning.

"Alimentary, my dear professor, alimentary," you answer.

All four of you burst into laughter. It feels good to be with your friends again.

Captain Bowman sees the injury on your arm and runs off to get you a bandage. Dr. Testoub then stands up and excuses herself to work on MultiFreak. She says she has a new idea. And Prof. Carcharias, pinching his nose and smiling, sends you off to the shower.

Afterward you rejoin Prof. Carcharias, and you're dying to find out exactly what happened.

"How did you know a flame would cause that?" you ask him.

"I didn't," he says. "It was just the first thing I thought of. I wanted you to disturb the stomach. You see, if a shark is bothered by something in its stomach, it has a most remarkable way of getting rid of it. As you experienced, it can lurch the stomach around, turn it inside-out—even thrust part of the lining through its mouth!"

Just then Prof. Carcharias is interrupted by a loud beeping noise. MultiFreak is going wild. Dr. Testoub is feverishly adjusting the controls.

"I think we've got it!" she says.

You and Prof. Carcharias run over to her, and you're joined by Captain Bowman, who helps you put on the bandage. Together you look out into the ocean.

About a hundred yards away, jumping and twisting in and out of the water, is a very energetic shark. Its bluish-gray body is jumping up so high, you can see its white underside. It's about five- or six-feet long, with a thick body and a pointed snout.

"It's a porbeagle shark," says Prof. Carcharias. "Strange . . . they don't usually exist this far south—and they certainly don't behave like that!"

"Well, it looks like this one has our box!" Dr. Testoub says. "What should we do now?"

■ Should you go closer and drop bait? Turn to page 72.

■ Should Captain Bowman harpoon it now? Turn to page 90.

You're fighting against the strength of a hungry shark. With each lurch of the stomach walls, your legs disappear into the spiral chamber. You can hear the sizzle as acid starts melting the leather on your shoes.

You let go with one hand and send out a signal with your video wrist monitor. Immediately it lights up, piercing through the blackness.

It's Prof. Carcharias. Even though the image is faint, you can see the shock on his face.

"Help me!" you cry.

"I don't believe it! You're still alive!" His voice sounds crackly; it's hard to hear.

"I'm in—"

He cuts you off. "We saw what happened—there's not enough time to talk! If you're inside the stomach, you've probably got very little air. Listen to me closely: *Light a match! I repeat: if you have an air bubble, light a match in it!"*

It sounds ridiculous, but you can't afford

to question him. You keep clutching the stomach wall with your wrist-monitor hand, and with the other you reach into your backpack. There are no matches, but there is a pocket lighter.

You hold it in the air bubble and flick it once, twice, three times. There are sparks, but no fire. Maybe there's not enough oxygen.

You flick it again. This time, the fuel ignites into a tiny flame. You adjust the nozzle on the lighter until the fire shoots up high and bright, touching the stomach wall.

It becomes harder to breathe each second as the lighter uses up your oxygen. You're starting to feel dizzy. There's a stinging sensation in your toes as the acid eats through your shoes. Your grip on the stomach wall is loosening.

This was a stupid idea. What did Prof. Carcharias have in mind anyway?

Suddenly you find out. The stomach wall starts convulsing violently. You're pulled away from the spiral chamber and jerked around with the other contents of the stomach.

At the same time, the lighter flickers off and your air gives out. You'll have to hold your breath as long as possible.

You may have been saved from digestion, but now you're being yanked around like a yo-yo! That TV set keeps banging into your head. You feel like the shark wants to snap you in two!

But just as you feel you're going to pass out, the stomach gives one sudden, enormous convulsion. Like a rubber band, the stomach wall snaps you through the opening, all the way up the gullet, and clear out of the shark's open mouth!

You splash out into the water, break through the surface, and gasp for breath. You feel like your lungs are going to burst. To your left, the great white shark turns tail on you and swims mightily out into the ocean. But to your right, you see nothing but the tall rocks. The *Survivor* is nowhere in sight. You thrash weakly in the water until you reach the rocks. You hold onto one and catch your breath. Has the *Survivor* sunk out of sight? Has it drifted miles away from you?

You sit on a rock and watch the seagulls dive-bomb into the water. You may have to wait here for hours or days, but you're happy to be alive. Exhausted, you lean back and fall asleep.

But you've barely started dreaming when a loud voice awakens you:

"All hands on deck! No loafing on duty!" It's Captain Bowman, yelling through a bullhorn on board the *Survivor*!

You rub your eyes in disbelief. Your

three shipmates are waving at you with huge smiles on their faces.

"Looks like ol' Great White swam you around to the other side of the rocks! We couldn't see you!" Captain Bowman calls out. "Got enough strength to swim out to us? We can't get much closer!"

You check the water for sharks and dive in. When you reach the ship, a rope cascades down over the side. You grab onto it with all your remaining strength as Captain Bowman happily pulls you up.

"You've truly gone where no person has gone before," Bowman calls down to you.

"Except maybe Jonah," you reply with a wink.

■ *Turn to page 80.*

"Here we go, hard to port!" Captain Bowman barks. He steers the ship south, well clear of the strange animal. You'll never know exactly what it was.

But the *Survivor* is facing another crisis now. Directly ahead is a long line of tall rocks. To avoid hitting them, Captain Bowman is staying a hard course to the south. But the current is strong, and it looks doubtful you'll make it.

You're distracted by Dr. Testoub, who's calling you from the stern hatchway. "Come down here!" she says. "I have to show you something!"

You follow her to the cargo hold, where she shows you a solid piece of metal, shaped like a giant arrowhead. It looks like it was pulled out of some sort of holder.

"Do you know what this is?" she asks.

"A letter opener for a brontosaurus?" you say.

"Don't be flip with me! I fail to find this humorous. This wasn't here before the shark attack."

"It's probably a spare part for Harpo or one of Captain Bowman's instruments. It could have even been a piece of scrap metal that was lodged in the shark's mouth before he crashed through. Sometimes they swallow crazy things."

"Perhaps . . . perhaps. . . ." Dr. Testoub seems disturbed. She walks out of the hold with you and paces the hallway.

"What's the matter?" you ask. "Still upset about that Elliot guy?"

"I suppose so," she says. "I spoke to him again today. He became angry with me when I insisted on continuing our search for Shark Chaser. Said CORD is running out of money, and the loss of Shark Chaser is the last straw. He wants to cut the company's losses. He'll give us one more day, and after that we're on our own."

You're about to console her, but you're both abruptly jolted against the wall. Scraping noises echo through the ship, and you rush up to the deck.

■ *Turn to page 67.*

"We've got him now!" says Captain Bowman. "And we know it's a shark this time! Let's harpoon it!"

You and he maneuver Harpo into place. It's going to be tough getting the porbeagle into the sight. It's jumping around like a marionette on a string. Captain Bowman holds on to the sight and moves it around to follow the shark.

"C'mon, baby ... stay still ... just a second ... take it easy ... OK ... *yeeaahhh!*"

He fires. The harpoon cuts through the air and meets its mark—just behind the porbeagle's gills.

But with a resounding *clang,* it bounces right off!

"I don't believe it," says Captain Bowman. "It's made of *metal!* It's a robot!"

You hear a sudden whoop from Dr. Testoub. "I thought so!" she yells. "Wahoooo!" You've never seen her this excited. She starts pulling crazily on MultiFreak's switches and knobs.

"I see," you say to her excitedly. "You're controlling its behavior!"

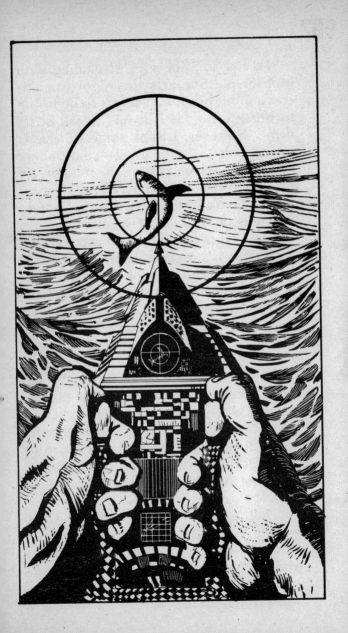

"I'd like to," she says, struggling with MultiFreak. She gets the robot to calm down a bit, but it still seems to be trying to break away, as if it had a will of its own. "However, I think someone else is trying to do the same thing—someone we can't see! Can you capture the robot while I still have it in my control?"

You have an idea. You turn to Captain Bowman and say, "Why don't we try Harpo again? This time you can wait till its mouth is open and aim the harpoon inside. Then it might hook onto something in there and we can pull it in."

Captain Bowman shakes his head. "Forget it. It'll just bounce off the metal again. I'm not in this business to ruin perfectly good expensive equipment!"

"Well, think of something, Popeye!" snaps Dr. Testoub. "If this thing swims off into the distance, so does your paycheck!"

Captain Bowman's face turns red with rage. "Just who do you think you're calling names? You've been nothing but trouble since we started, and I have half a mind to—"

"Half a mind is right!" Dr. Testoub retorts. All of her bottled-up anger for Bowman spills out. "I've had enough of your witless insults and your incompetent seamanship! You've almost gotten us killed more times than I can count, and now you're willing to watch the world's first shark repellent float away into some criminal's hands!"

"Listen, you, I don't need some hysterical landlubber telling me how to run my ship!"

"Oliver, Vivian! Please!" Prof. Carcharias interrupts, trying to make peace. "Let us not forget we are professionals!"

As the three of them go at it, you realize you're on your own.

■ *Use Harpo yourself and follow your own plan. Turn to page 103.*

■ *Put on the chain-mail suit and go after the metal shark. Turn to page 99.*

The stomach walls are pulling you into the spiral chamber with tremendous force. You're already in up to your kneecaps. You feel the leather on your shoes start to sizzle.

With all your strength, you dig your hands into the soft stomach wall. It's slippery, but you're able to grab handholds. You pull yourself up, inch by inch. But each time your feet pull clear of the intestine, the stomach walls squeeze you back down.

You grab tighter, determined to try again, but you sense that your worst fear is coming true. It's becoming much harder to breathe; you're using up your air bubble.

You make one more mighty pull—and yank your body back into the shark's stomach.

Your air is gone now. You have to hold your breath; that'll give you only a minute or two. You grope for the opening to the gullet. Maybe you can crawl back out through the mouth.

Suddenly the stomach gives a violent lurch. You're tossed helplessly end-over-end into the back of the stomach. And you disappear into the spiral chamber, a lively dinner for a hungry shark.

THE END

It's completely dark. You're sliding down a long, warm tube. The walls of the tube are wet and fleshy. You know you're alive, because you can still feel the pain in your arm.

With horror, you realize you're inside the gullet of the great white shark. The walls are squeezing in and out, forcing you downward. You hear a dull pumping—that must be the gills of the shark, opening and closing in the water.

You're still breathing and in one piece. You were lucky—when the shark swallowed you he also gulped down a pocket of air. But that won't hold out for long.

You have no idea how you can possibly escape. How did Jonah get out of the whale? Maybe if *he* did it, there's a way . . .

But your thoughts are rudely interrupted. You pass through some kind of opening and tumble into a large, pitch-dark, foul-smelling cavern. This has got to be the stomach. You land on your side—right on top of a metal box! Could this be the Chaser-Tracer Box? You feel all around it until there's no doubt in your mind what it is—a TV set! The shark must have swallowed it from some capsized pleasure boat.

All around, you feel objects you wouldn't expect to be here: pieces of driftwood, rope, a pair of pants, an umbrella. There are also some cold, clammy things you don't even want to guess about!

But the stomach is supposed to be for digestion—it's where body acids break down food. So why aren't you and all of these other things being burned up by digestive juices?

Of course! You remember from your pre-trip briefing that a shark's stomach is different from a human's. It's little more than a holding pouch. If a shark doesn't feel like digesting something it swallowed, it can just store it in the stomach for days or weeks! Whatever it wants to digest passes into the intestine. That's where the real danger is.

The intestine has a tight, spiral-shaped valve. When food travels through the spiral, it's splashed with acid and digested. No one knows how sharks choose which foods to store in the stomach and which to digest.

All at once you're gripped with fear.

You have the feeling you've been "chosen" for a trip to the intestine. The stomach walls begin moving around you, turning you around and inching you further along. Soon your feet are going through an opening, into an area that makes a churning sound.

There's no time to lose. Your air bubble is running out, and you're about to become shark nutrients.

You realize you're still wearing your underwater video wrist monitor. You reach for it—but what possible good could it do you now? Even if you had time to radio for help, what could anyone do except say good-bye?

■ *Forget the monitor; use both hands to climb back up the stomach wall. Turn to page 94.*

■ *Take your chances and radio for help. Turn to page 83.*

As the three of them argue, you look out into the sea. The robot is spinning around and making whirring noises. It sounds like its motor is wearing out from the strain. You wonder if it's like a real shark—if it stops, will it sink?

This may be your last chance to recover the Chaser-Tracer Box. You go over to a storage bin and take out the chain-mail suit. The robot's jaw has sharp metal teeth; they may be capable of cutting through the suit, but you've got to give it a try.

You climb into the suit, fasten breathing apparatus onto your back, and clamp the helmet in place. Then you attach a specially designed pontoon so you won't sink to the bottom. None of your shipmates sees you as you dive in.

You swim slowly toward the robot. It's hard to figure out how to handle it. For a moment it seems to just sit silently in the water, and then without warning it flips into the air.

When it settles again, you reach for its dorsal fin. The robot shakes from side to side, clipping you in the helmet with its tail.

Then it rolls lazily around in the water. You quickly grab one of its flippers with your left hand. A *clank* rings out as metal slaps metal. You've finally got the robot to stop fighting.

Or so you think. Before you can react, the robot spins around and clamps its jaw into your right shoulder.

Fortunately, the teeth don't penetrate your suit. But the jaw is locked shut. Wiggling your way out is impossible. Your arms hang out helplessly in the water. You hear the radio signals from the Chaser-Tracer Box inside the robot—just a few feet away from you. If you could only . . .

There does seem to be a possibility. Even though the robot has your shoulder, you can still move your arms. You swing your right hand up and grab onto the partially open jaw. Then you struggle to pivot your arm around. The metal of your suit squeaks against the robot's teeth as you slowly move your arm into its mouth. Your forearm enters, but your elbow is stuck.

Finally, with a mighty yank you thrust your whole arm into the mouth. You stretch

down until your fingertips just touch the long-lost Chaser-Tracer Box.

Just then the robot opens its mouth— and you fall further in! The robot clamps down again, this time around your waist. Now your upper body is inside the metallic monster and your legs are dangling out.

But you have the box. You have it firmly in your hands.

You just have to think of a way to get out of here.

■ *Turn to page 105.*

You glance out to the robot shark. Its jaws are snapping open and shut. Inside its mouth you can make out a network of wires, bolts, and panels. If you could just get a harpoon lodged in there, it would be a piece of cake to pull the shark in.

The three others are still arguing. This is your chance. You sneak over to Harpo and look through the sight. The robot has started moving more wildly, now that Dr. Testoub is distracted. You try to keep it in your sight as it jumps in the air, turns its back to you, and plunges into the water. This is going to be tough.

You wait for it to emerge again. It flails around and then reaches its gaping mouth high above the surface of the water. You've got it now . . .

"Hey! What do you think you're doing?" Captain Bowman's voice booms out. You've been discovered.

You fire into the robot's open mouth. The harpoon darts right in—and it rips through the other side, tearing the robot in two!

The inner circuitry of the robot spills out into the water. And before it all sinks away, you catch your first—and last—glimpse of the Chaser-Tracer Box.

THE END

It may not be the insides of a great white shark this time, but you feel just as trapped. The robot tosses its head to one side and your helmet crashes against one of the curved inner walls of its body. You find yourself staring at a symbol stamped into the metal:

You memorize it; it may be a clue to the identity of the criminals.

The robot lifts itself up again. But this time it doesn't come down. In fact, you feel yourself being lifted clear out of the water.

"We've got you, kid! Just can't keep you away from those shark innards, can we?"

Through a corner of the robot's jaw, you can see that you're being pulled up in a huge fishing net with the ship's crane.

You're hoisted over the ship railing, still halfway in the mouth of the robot.

You land on the deck of the *Survivor*, and your shipmates use crowbars to try to pry you loose.

Nothing seems to work, until Dr. Testoub wedges something that looks like a car jack between the jaw. She pumps and pumps—and you finally squeeze out.

"Uh, nice work, Doctor," Captain Bowman says quietly. He gives Dr. Testoub a weak smile as Prof. Carcharias helps you off with your suit.

"Here's where the congratulations should go, once again," Prof. Carcharias says, patting you on the shoulder. "This youngster has saved our lives *and* rescued our project when we couldn't even be civil to one another."

"Hey, no sweat," you say as you show the Chaser-Tracer Box to Dr. Testoub. From the look on her face when she sees it, you're not sure if she's happier to see you or the box!

"I'll let you have it on one condition," you tell her. "You have to explain how you knew the shark was a robot."

Dr. Testoub laughs and says, "Well, I first got the idea from one of the first things you said when you came on board. You asked if a *criminal* could have sent a shark. We laughed at that. A shark could

never follow those instructions—a *real* shark, that is. That got me to thinking. Then there was that triangular piece of metal in the cargo hold."

"A metal version of a shark tooth!" you say.

"Exactly! So I surmised the shark was a robot, and it was undoubtedly heading straight back to its launching pad. I then figured it might be radio-controlled, so I used MultiFreak to find its signal and jam it."

"What a brain!" you say. "But answer me one question. What does this symbol mean? I saw it stamped inside the robot." You draw the symbol you saw:

"That's the CORD company logo!" Prof. Carcharias says.

"Which confirms my final suspicion," says Dr. Testoub. "After all those years that CORD supported us, I couldn't understand why Elliot Brine, that new director, would want to cut our funds—"

"Unless he was part of the criminal ring who wanted Shark Chaser!" Captain Bowman cuts in. Dr. Testoub gives him a sharp look for interrupting. "Oh, excuse me, Doctor," Bowman says, with unusual respect for his shipmate. He's obviously impressed by what Dr. Testoub has done.

"So, you see," Dr. Testoub continues, "we have you to thank—for your ideas and your deeds!"

"Thanks, kid," says Captain Bowman, "Too bad there aren't any medals for what you did."

Both Dr. Testoub and Prof. Carcharias break into grins and nod in agreement.

"Oh, it's no big deal. Really," you say modestly.

As Captain Bowman points the *Survivor* back toward the mainland, you're proud to have been the one to recover Shark Chaser. Because of you, many lives will be saved from killer sharks.

But Bowman's last comment sticks in your mind. You have to admit you were hoping for *something* to show for it. Looks like you'll just have to settle for those black-and-blue marks.

 THE END

TOP SECRET

The following brief contains information that may be essential to a successful completion of your assignment.

1. There are 250 species of shark. Of these, about 35 are man-eaters. Man-eaters include the great white shark, the great hammerhead, the tiger shark, the porbeagle, and the mako. Sharks harmless to humans include the whale shark and the basking shark, both of which sift plankton by means of their gills.

2. Sharks can detect their prey in several ways: they can see it (and have good vision in the dark); they can smell fish oil or blood a quarter mile away (or much longer on a current); they can hear low-frequency noises, such as the fluttering of fish (or humans) in the water. They also have special electrically sensitive pores near the snout that can detect the natural electrical fields of living things—with these pores, they can find a flatfish buried in sand!

3. When sharks smell fish oil or blood in the water, they sometimes go into a "feeding frenzy." They lurch around violently, biting at anything around them—including other sharks!

4. If a shark loses a tooth, another one grows in to take its place. Behind the main row of teeth, as many as five extra rows lie inside the gum, waiting for action.

5. Water must pump through a shark's gills in order for it to absorb oxygen from the water. Some sharks can pump their own gills open and shut, or *ventilate* them. But most can't—they must constantly keep swimming to force water through.

6. Sharks cannot swim backward. If they swim into a net, chances are they will be stuck. Then, since they also can't swim forward to ventilate their gills, they'll drown. In Sydney, Australia in 1937, loose-hanging nets were placed in the water each night to protect bathing beaches. In the first year of this plan, 1,500 sharks were caught in the nets.

7. Since sharks do not have air bladders like many other fish, they will sink to the bottom if they stop swimming. Sharks who can ventilate their own gills often

rest at the bottom of the sea. All others must keep swimming without stopping their whole lives—even while sleeping!

8. A shark's stomach is a mysterious thing. It can store food *without digesting it* for days or weeks. If a shark doesn't like something in its stomach, the shark can turn the stomach inside out, and actually send part of the lining back up its throat and even through its mouth to spit the object out.

9. Sharks are fish; porpoises are mammals. Shark brains have highly developed instincts; porpoise brains have highly developed intelligence, too. If a pack of sharks attacks a prey, each one fights individually. If a pack of porpoises confronts a shark, they work together to defeat it.

10. A shark's skin feels smooth if you rub it one way—but rub it the other way and you may cut your hand. It's covered with sharp edges known as "skin teeth."

11. Basking sharks travel slowly and in schools. They have the habit of lining up practically nose-to-tail, so a line of them looks like one long sea serpent from a distance!

12. Although lots have been tested, there has never been any effective shark repellent developed. Only one foolproof shark poison is known to exist, a natural substance manufactured by a fish called the Moses sole.

END BRIEF.

■ You are ready to return to your assignment. Turn to page 1.

The Contributors

PETER LERANGIS is an author, actor, singer, and teacher. He has had over a dozen books published, including Time Traveler #4, *The Amazing Ben Franklin.* Recently he wrote storybook adaptations for the movies *Young Sherlock Holmes, Little Shop of Horrors,* and *Star Trek IV.* He has been in the Broadway show *They're Playing Our Song* and has played lead roles in many shows throughout the country.

WALTER P. MARTISHIUS is a book illustrator, theatrical set designer, and a production designer and art director for films. He is the illustrator of Time Machine #10, *American Revolutionary;* Explorer #1, *Journey to the Center of the Atom;* and Explorer #2, *Destination: Brain.*